Nikki

MARISABINA RUSSO

Where Is Ben?

Greenwillow Books New York

Gouache paints were used for the full-color art.
The text type is Kabel Medium.

Printed in Hong Kong by South China Printing Company (1988) Ltd.

First Edition 10 9 8 7 6 5 4 3 2 1

Library of Congress Cataloging-in-Publication Data

Russo, Marisabina.
Where is Ben? / Marisabina Russo.
p.   cm.
Summary: While Ben's mother makes a pie,
Ben hides around the house.
ISBN 0-688-08011-1. ISBN 0-688-08013-8 (lib. bdg.)
[1. Hide-and-seek—Fiction.]   I. Title.
PZ7.R9192Wg   1990
[E]—dc19   88-34916   CIP   AC

For the

whole gang:
_____

AMBER,

BEN,

CASSIDY,

HANNAH,

SAM,

and

SLADE

Ben's mother was busy making an apple pie. "Won't you help me roll out the dough?" she asked Ben.

"No," said Ben. "I'm going to hide, and you won't find me."

Ben's mother patted and rolled the dough. Then she heard a faraway voice calling, "Mama, come find me."

There was a coat rack in one corner of the kitchen. A hat and coat had fallen on the floor next to it. Ben's mother stared at the coat rack.

"Where is Ben?" she asked, lifting the edge of a hanging coat.

"You found me!" squealed Ben.

"Yes, I did," said Ben's mother. "Now let's pick up this coat and hat and hang them up again."

Ben's mother continued making apple pie. When she had all the apples peeled she heard a faraway voice calling, "Mama, come find me."

Ben's mother went out into the living room. There was a mess of laundry on the floor next to the upside-down laundry basket.

Ben's mother tapped on the side of the basket. "Where is Ben?" she asked as she turned it over.

"You found me!" squealed Ben.

"Yes, I did," said Ben's mother. "Now let's hide the laundry back in the basket."

Then she said, "I'm almost finished making the pie. When I put it in the oven I will read you a story, and then it will be time for your nap."

Ben's mother had just spread the top crust over the apples when she heard a faraway voice calling, "Mama, come find me."

Ben's mother looked in the hall. She saw a jumble of boots on the floor next to the coat closet. She rapped on the door.

"Where is Ben?" she asked as she opened the door.

"You found me!" squealed Ben.

"Yes, I did," said Ben's mother. "Now let's hide the boots back in the closet."

Then she said, "All I have to do is cut a flower in the crust, and then it will be time for your story and your nap."

Just when Ben's mother had put the pie in the oven
she heard a faraway voice calling, "Mama, come
find me."

Ben's mother looked in the kitchen, the living room, and the hallway, but she could not find Ben.
"Where is Ben?" she called loudly.
"Mama, come find me." The faraway voice was coming from upstairs.

In Ben's room she saw all his dolls on the floor next to his bed. She patted the blanket.

"Where is Ben?" she asked as she pulled back the covers.

"You found me!" squealed Ben.

"Yes, I did," said Ben's mother. "Now let's hide all the dolls and you too in your cozy bed, and then we'll read a story before your nap."

"And when I wake up we can eat some apple pie!" said Ben.